To those who seek light in the darkness — JEB
A million times for my mother — SS

Groundwood Books / House of Anansi Press
groundwoodbooks.com

We acknowledge for their financial support of our publishing program the Canada Council for
the Arts, the Ontario Arts Council and the Government of Canada.

Canada Council   Conseil des Arts
for the Arts   du Canada

ONTARIO ARTS COUNCIL
CONSEIL DES ARTS DE L'ONTARIO
an Ontario government agency
un organisme du gouvernement de l'Ontario

With the participation of the Government of Canada
Avec la participation du gouvernement du Canada   Canadä

Library and Archives Canada Cataloguing in Publication
Bogart, Jo Ellen, author
The white cat and the monk : a retelling of the poem Pangur
Bán / Jo Ellen Bogart ; pictures by Sydney Smith.
A retelling of the anonymous Irish poem Pangur Bán.
Issued in print and electronic formats.
ISBN 978-1-55498-780-1 (bound). —ISBN 978-1-55498-781-8 (pdf)
1. Monks—Juvenile fiction. 2. Cats—Juvenile fiction. 3. Truth—
Juvenile fiction. I. Smith, Sydney, illustrator II. Title.
PS8553.O465W45 2016   jC813'.54   C2015-903291-1
C2015-903293-8

The illustrations were done in watercolor and ink.
Design by Michael Solomon
Printed and bound in Malaysia

the White Cat
and the
Monk

A Retelling of the Poem
"Pangur Bán"

Jo Ellen Bogart

illustrations by
Sydney Smith

Groundwood Books
House of Anansi Press
Toronto Berkeley

I, monk and scholar,

share my room

with my white cat, Pangur.

By candle's light, late into the night,

we work, each at a special trade.

Far more than any fame, I enjoy the peaceful pursuit of knowledge.

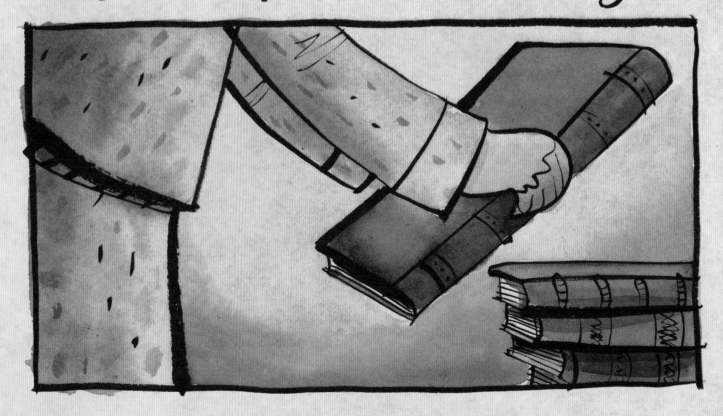

I treasure the wealth to be found in my books.

Pangur has his own pursuit,
his game of chase and catch.

The silent hunter, he sits and
stares at the wall.

He studies the hole
that leads to the
mouse's home.

My own eyes, older and
less bright than his,

study my manuscript,
hunting for meaning.

Each page is a challenge.

Pangur does not disturb me
at my work,

and I do not disturb him
at his.

We are each content, with all
we need to entertain us.

Ours is a happy tale.

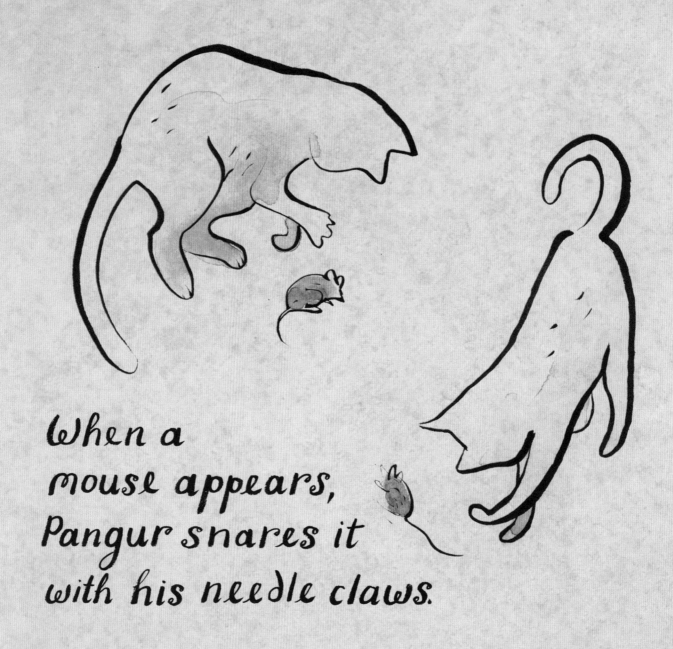

When a
mouse appears,
Pangur snares it
with his needle claws.

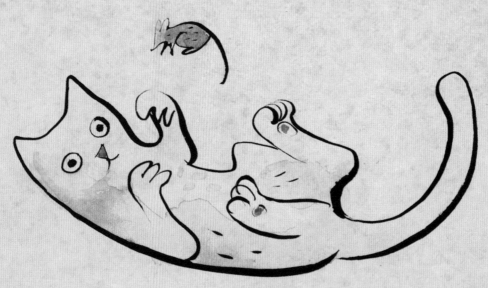

He feels joy at catching his prey.

I feel joy as I find, at last,
the answer to my puzzle.

In our tiny home,
Pangur finds his mouse...

Author's Note

More than one thousand years ago, in the ninth century, an Irish Benedictine monk, whose name has never been uncovered, stopped in his studies to write down his thoughts. In Old Irish, in rhyming couplets, he described his companion, a white cat who shared his small room. He found similarities in their pastimes. Each was seeking something.

Was the monk hoping to share his thoughts with someone who would read his poem? Was his imagination enhanced by the candle flame dancing in the darkness of the night? Amidst his study of the words of others, did he take pleasure in creating something of his own?

The monk probably wrote the poem while staying at the Reichenau Abbey, in southern Germany, or in the nearby region. The notebook containing the poem was given the name *Reichenau Primer* and can now be found in the monastery of St. Paul in Carinthia, in Austria.

The poem, called "Pangur Bán," is a peek into the time and mind of one poet. It has been translated many times by various people and has become well known and loved. In this book, the words have been inspired by a number of translations written over many years. The story of the monk and his cat can also be seen as a timeless tale that is played out again and again all over the world wherever a person is at work accompanied by a beloved pet.

In Irish, the word *bán* means white. Pangur has been said to refer to the word *fuller*, a person who fluffed and whitened cloth. We might think, then, that Pangur Bán was a cat with brilliantly white fur. Perhaps he even glowed in the candlelight.